THE WIT OF TENAL

Devika Rangachari h...
competitions for writer...
book, *Growing Up* (C... was
nominated to the Honou... ...al Board
on Books for Young Peop... ...2 as the most
outstanding Indian entry. Her o... ...ks include *Company
for Manisha* (CBT, 1999), *When An...na Went Away* (CBT, 2002),
Stories from Rajatarangini—Tales of Kashmir (CBT, 2001) and
Stories from Kathasaritsagara (CBT, 2003).

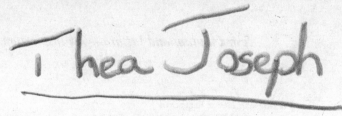

Thea Joseph

The Wit of Tenali Raman

Devika Rangachari

Illustrations Shilpa Ranade

SCHOLASTIC
New York Toronto London Auckland
Sydney New Delhi Hong Kong

'For Gautam and Uttara—my inspiration,
my world'

Text © 2007 Devika Rangachari
Illustrations © 2007 Scholastic India Pvt Ltd

Published by Scholastic India Pvt. Ltd.
A subsidiary of Scholastic Inc., New York, 10012 (USA).
Publishers since 1920, with international operations in Canada, Australia, New
Zealand, the United Kingdom, India and Hong Kong.

For information regarding permission, write to:
Scholastic India Pvt. Ltd.
Golf View Corporate Tower-A, 3rd Floor,
DLF Phase-V, Gurgaon 122002 (India)

Typeset by Mantra Virtual Services Pvt Ltd

First edition: January 2007

Reprinted : February, March, August, Oct., 2007
January, February, April 2008; Sep., Nov., 2009;
February 2010 Jun 2010 Aug. 2010 May September 2017

ISBN-13: 978-81-7655-603-3

Printed at: Ram Printograph, Delhi

Contents

Note on Tenali Raman and the Sources

Tenali Raman, who lived in the early sixteenth century, is regarded as one of the most popular folk figures in India today. Also dubbed 'the Birbal of the South', Raman was the royal jester at the court of Krishna Devaraya (A.D.1509-1529) of Vijayanagara in Andhra Pradesh. It was under Krishna Devaraya's rule that the Vijayanagara empire, one of the most famous empires in the history of southern India, is considered to have reached its peak. The king himself was a mighty warrior who rarely lost a battle but treated his enemies with honour. Tenali Raman was one of the *ashtadiggajas* or eight poets of great stature at his court. Not only was he a great Telugu poet, he was also notable for his knowledge, wit and ingenuity.

Although some scholars contend that Tenali Raman was only a boy at the time of Krishna

Devaraya's reign, his historicity as the court jester is generally accepted. In fact, the famous traveller, Domingo Paes, confirms the image of the king that arises from the stories. He says that Krishna Devaraya was 'most feared' but a 'perfect king', and that he was 'cheerful of disposition and very merry'. Paes notes, however, that although the king was 'a great ruler and a man of much justice', he was subject to 'sudden fits of rage'. Krishna Devaraya was also a contemporary of the Mughal emperor Babur and of King Henry VIII of England.

Although stories and legends concerning Tenali Raman are usually presented in a disjointed fashion, it is possible to link up the tales in a connected narrative so as to provide a picture of the amazing ingenuity and resourcefulness of this man, and the influence he wielded over Krishna Devaraya and his court. In fact, stories gleaned from different sources seem to corroborate each other on the main aspects of Raman's life and on the legends that surrounded him, thereby lending a note of authenticity to the tales. However, the exact historical value of specific stories has not been established.

Raman was supposed to have been born in the small village of Garlapadu in the Guntur district of Andhra Pradesh. He was named after the deity of the great Ramalingeswara temple in Tenali by his maternal uncle who took care of the boy and his mother after Raman's father died of cholera. Admittedly, Raman was acknowledged and lauded for his cleverness and wit. However, he was also a great poet, one of his most famous works being the epic *Panduranga Mahatmyam*. Legend has it that Raman had many children with Mangamma and lived a long and fruitful life, dying unexpectedly of a snake-bite soon after his return from Babur's court and casting Krishna Devaraya into deep depression thereby.

The sources used for this book include:

Tenali Rama by P. Ayyar, The Orient Publishing Co., Madras/Hyderabad, 1957.

Stories of Tenali Raman by C.L.L. Jayaprada, Children's Book Trust, New Delhi, 2001.

Stories/articles on Tenali Raman and Krishna Devaraya in the *Amar Chitra Katha* series and in historical works.

Two Boons

However enraged Raman's victims were, after one look at his bright eyes and plump cheeks, they would invariably forget their wrath and say, 'Oh, run away, you naughty boy! And don't you dare play a prank on me again!'

Raman would run off to find his next victim or stretch out under his favourite palmyra tree for a satisfying snooze. At the end of each day, he trudged home to his mother, who wrung her hands at her son's misdeeds and wondered what he would make of his life.

There was no doubt that Raman was smart. From the time that his uncle had brought his widowed sister and her son back to his village, Tenali, little Ramalinga, or Raman as he was usually called, had delighted his elders by his intelligence. But he had as swiftly exasperated them by his love for mischief.

Every day posed a new trial for his teacher, who found that no amount of cajoling, threatening or beating would quell the high-spirited boy. 'Not only is he impossibly mischievous,' complained the teacher to Raman's uncle, 'but he is also unbearably lazy. He can put his mind to anything if he wants to, but he chooses not to.'

'What will become of him?' queried the anxious uncle, who strove to hide his fondness for his nephew under a gruff exterior. 'Is there no hope?'

'None at all,' said the teacher grimly. 'He will be the world's greatest prankster and idler. On the other hand,' he added quickly, seeing the uncle's face fall, 'you can pray for a miracle. Perhaps he will be a great man some day.'

Raman's uncle died when Raman was still very young, and the boy and his mother lived lives of extreme poverty and hardship. Yet Raman showed no signs of reforming his ways, and his tomfoolery reached new heights.

That year, there was a drought. The citizens of

Tenali searched the sky with anxious eyes for signs of rain, as the land grew more and more parched. Finally, when all hope seemed lost, a venerable old man, a sanyasi, entered the village. Soon after, there was rain.

The people of Tenali danced about wildly with cries of joy and relief. The sanyasi was proclaimed a saviour and a miracle-man. Everyone was awed by the magic he had wrought.

Everyone, that is, except Raman. The boy went up to the sanyasi and said, 'How's the old palmyra tree?' The sanyasi nodded appreciatively but everyone else looked completely mystified.

As Raman turned and was walking away, a friend accosted him. 'What did you mean by that?'

'It's simple,' answered Raman. 'A crow sat on a branch of the palmyra tree and a fruit fell down. Everyone immediately thought that the bird had done it. It's the same with this sanyasi—he enters the village and it rains, so everyone thinks he's brought it about. People!' Raman grimaced.

'Quite right,' said an amused voice behind him. It was the sanyasi. His friend turned tail and ran but Raman stood his ground. 'My boy,' the sanyasi went on, 'I really appreciate your bright face and quick wit. What do you do for a living?'

Raman could hardly say that he spent a large part

of his day sleeping, so he lied with as straight a face as he could muster. 'I don't have very good health,' he began.

'Oh, that is terrible,' the sanyasi sounded deeply concerned. 'Well, I'm going to help a deserving boy like you. I will teach you a *mantra* to invoke goddess Kali. Sit in her temple tonight and recite it. When she comes before you, ask boldly for what you want.'

Raman was instantly curious. Was the sanyasi serious about this?

That night Raman made his way to the small Kali temple near his house. There was not a soul in sight but, even so, he closed the doors after he went in so as to remain unobserved. Then he began chanting the *mantra*.

It felt a little eerie at first, chanting loudly in the dark with no one to hear or see him but an unmoving idol. Nevertheless, he kept at it and was rewarded in a most spectacular fashion.

Just as he had chanted Kali's name a hundred thousand times, there appeared a frightening figure before him. It was the goddess with her thousand heads. Her eyes were huge and fiery, and blood dripped off her tongues.

Raman stared at the apparition with wide eyes. Kali stared back at him fiercely.

Then, most unexpectedly, Raman burst out

laughing. His guffaws filled the room and tears of merriment rolled down his cheeks.

The goddess' expression changed. People swooned, cried and trembled at her appearance but no one had ever laughed. 'Why do you laugh?' she demanded—and her voice was deep and awe-inspiring.

'Forgive me, O goddess,' gasped Raman, wiping away his tears and trying to speak steadily, 'but I suddenly wondered what you would do if you caught a cold. I have such a problem with just one nose dripping—but you have a thousand!'

Kali's eyes glowed red with anger. What impudence! Then, all at once, she too began to laugh—and she kept it up for so long that Raman began to get a little worried.

At length, she stopped and looked at Raman with affection.

'You *vikatakavi*!' she said. 'You have no idea how long it is since someone dared to joke with me. It feels good to laugh.'

'I like the title, clever buffoon,' said Raman, relieved. 'It reads the same from either end. I couldn't have asked for anything better.'

Kali impulsively held out two golden bowls, one in either hand. 'Look, Raman,' she said. 'The bowl in my right hand has the sweet milk of learning while the one in my left has the sour curds of wealth. Choose one and you shall have it.'

Raman considered a while. This was a difficult choice. Knowledge or wealth? Should he choose the left or the right? Aloud he said, 'Mother, why is wealth associated with sour curd?'

'Because wealth is hardly ever acquired by pleasant means,' retorted Kali.

Raman made up his mind. 'How can I choose, O Kali, without tasting them both?' he asked.

'All right, taste a bit of both,' offered the goddess.

Before she quite knew what was happening, Raman had gulped down the contents of both bowls. The goddess' eyes began to glow with rage.

'Forgive me,' Raman said penitently to the irate goddess. 'I had to have both. One without the other would have been useless to me.'

'You imp!' exclaimed Kali, torn between anger and laughter. 'You disobeyed me and will have to pay for this. So while you will be a great poet, you will be better known as a jester—for that is what comes naturally to you. And your prosperity will bring you several enemies—but with my blessings, you will outwit them each time.'

Then, with a parting smile as she remembered Raman's first comments, Kali disappeared into thin air.

Raman was thrilled beyond measure. He mumbled his thanks to the space where she had been, and left the temple to lie under his favourite palmyra tree.

As Raman lay in the darkness, he could hardly believe his luck. All at once, Tenali seemed too small a place for a man of his learning and ability. But where could he go?

The solution struck him quite suddenly. He would go to Vijayanagara, to the court of Krishna Devaraya. The king was famous for promoting poets and writers, and for surrounding himself with people of intelligence and merit. He was apparently a very generous patron but there was a flip side too—one for which he was equally famous. The king's temper was said to be frightening. In a bad mood, he could fling around death sentences like breeze scattering pollen in the air.

Lying under his tree, Raman smiled confidently to himself. He had his boons and he would succeed.

Going to Court

Raman lost no time in telling everyone about his plans. His friends jeered at him while his mother, used to Raman's unpredictable ways, made no comment.

One difficulty, however, struck Raman. How could he barge into Krishna Devaraya's court without a patron or a recommendation?

While pondering on a solution, Raman married Mangamma, a distant relative, much to the amazement of his friends and the delight of his mother.

Shortly after Raman's wedding, Tatachari, the pompous royal priest at Krishna Devaraya's court, came to worship at the shrine of Mangalagiri near Tenali. When Raman heard of this, he decided that here lay the solution to his problem.

Raman lost no time in ingratiating himself with the priest. He fetched and carried and served Tatachari every day. When the day for the priest's departure dawned, Tatachari, possibly out of a desire to show Raman how powerful he was at court, said that whenever Raman wanted a job at the Vijayanagara court, he had only to ask him.

Even before the dust raised by Tatachari's carriage had settled, Raman was scampering home to ask his mother and wife to pack all their belongings.

They left the following morning, and after a wearying journey of many days, reached the great city.

Raman feasted his eyes on the broad streets, the huge shops, the massive temples, the displays of jewellery and silk, and the majestic elephants and chariots. He rejoiced at the amazing turn his fortunes had taken.

When Raman presented himself at Tatachari's house, however, he was not granted an audience. 'He must be tired after his journey,' thought Raman cheerfully and resolved to come back the following day.

Yet he faced the same refusal the next morning, and the next, and the next. Tatachari's good intentions had clearly been shorter than the journey between Tenali and Vijayanagara. Finally one day, one of the guards told him that Tatachari had no idea who he was and he should cease to bother him.

Hurt and bewildered, Raman refused to be defeated by this obstacle. He dug out his best clothes and made his way to Krishna Devaraya's court.

As it happened, that morning there was a great debate between scholars on the reality of objective phenomena. As a result, the main hall was thronged with people from many cities who had been invited to watch the battle of wits. No guards questioned the stranger as he managed to slip in with the other invitees. Raman's luck seemed to be finally turning.

Though it was hard to stop staring at the grand room with its ornate ceiling and decorated pillars, and to focus on two short, fat men arguing doggedly, Raman tried his best. He kept getting distracted by trying to catch glimpses of Krishna Devaraya, and by imagining himself as one of the grandly dressed men sitting by the king, occasionally leaning forward to hear his comments.

When he finally managed to focus his attention on the debate again, one scholar was insisting that the world was an illusion. 'It is our thoughts alone that make us think we are seeing, hearing, tasting, smelling and touching things,' he declared grandly.

The perplexity on everyone's face was evident, but they all applauded politely as the scholar sat down with a satisfied air.

Raman could not contain himself. Pushing himself to the front of the crowd, he said loudly, 'Sir, is there no difference between our eating a thing and thinking that we are eating it?'

'None,' replied the scholar.

'In that case,' said Raman boldly, addressing the audience at large, 'let's test this man's theory. Let's all eat the rich feast provided by the king and let this man think that he is eating it and fill his stomach.'

A roar of appreciative laughter followed.

Raman suddenly found himself face-to-face with the king. For the first time in his life, he found himself stammering slightly while introducing himself to the impressive, dignified figure before him whose eyes gleamed with genuine enjoyment. Would the king be angry at his cheeky intrusion? Had he overstepped some line or the other? Then he became aware that the king was addressing him.

'Raman of Tenali,' said Krishna Devaraya, holding out a purse of gold, 'I am pleased by your wit. You will be my court jester from now on. Take this money and buy yourself a house and whatever else you need.'

A thrill of triumph shot through Raman and sudden tears filled his eyes. It had been a long journey to his goal, and one that had been fraught with uncertainty. And he had sometimes wondered whether he was merely chasing an illusion. Yet it had been worth it for, at long last, his dream had been fulfilled and that was all that mattered.

 # The Biter Bit

It was a brand-new life for Raman. He was the jester at the famed court of Krishna Devaraya. He lived in a splendid house, wore the best clothes and ate the choicest food. Yet, try as he might, he could not forget Tatachari's betrayal.

The old priest had been shocked and dismayed at Raman's appointment as jester. At the time of the announcement, he had to pull his features hurriedly into a smile, hoping that his annoyance did not show. He had consoled himself with the thought that Raman was new to court ways and that he could easily use the latter's inexperience to embarrass him. But Raman was a fast learner and, in no time at all, it seemed as if he had always lived at the court.

As the weeks passed, Tatachari hardly bothered to mask his hostility towards the jester. For the most part, he pretended as if Raman did not exist, and when circumstances forced him to acknowledge his existence, he called him 'Jester' and pretended to forget his name.

Raman pondered ways and means to make the priest pay for his duplicity. He knew he was treading dangerous ground here for Krishna Devaraya treated Tatachari with great respect. Yet he could not still his irrepressible urge for revenge.

At long last, an opportunity presented itself. Raman, by dint of patient spying, discovered that Tatachari often bathed alone in a pool in the Tungabhadra, three miles from the town, at about four in the morning. He would bathe naked, keeping his clothes on the bank.

One morning, Raman followed the priest to the pool as noiselessly as he could,—no mean task in itself considering his rather portly figure. Hiding behind a tree on the bank, he waited till Tatachari entered the pool. He then crept forward, gathered up the priest's clothes and deposited them behind the tree.

A short while later, his ablutions completed, Tatachari climbed back on to the bank. As he stood shivering in the cold morning air, he discovered to his amazement and annoyance that his clothes were missing. What made him feel even more chagrinned was the sight of Raman, leaning negligently against a tree and eyeing him with frank curiosity.

'Where are my clothes?' demanded the deeply embarrassed priest.

'Oh, so you deign to speak to me now?' remarked Raman.

'Give me back my clothes, Raman!' said Tatachari firmly.

'All this while, you could hardly ever remember me or my name. I wonder now why that was!' said Raman meditatively.

'Give me back my clothes!' said Tatachari in increasing desperation.

'Your clothes?' retorted Raman. 'What would I know about your clothes? And why would you be wandering around here without your clothes, in any case?'

Back and forth the argument swung, and Tatachari's pleas became more desperate and Raman's responses more frivolous.

At long last, the old priest threw up his hands. 'I give up, Raman. Tell me what you want and I'll do it.

But please, I beg you, give me back my clothes. It's getting late and I need to be at the palace.'

Raman smiled broadly. 'All you need to do,' he said, 'is carry me to the palace square on your shoulders.'

'I'll do it!' shouted Tatachari. 'Now give me back my clothes.'

Shortly thereafter, a curious procession entered the town. At its head was Tatachari with Raman comfortably perched on his shoulders. A noisy crowd, composed mostly of excited children, followed them, cheering loudly and shouting words of encouragement.

Hearing the din from the terrace of his palace, Krishna Devaraya leaned out and saw the look of misery on Tatachari's face and that of triumph on Raman's. His famous temper stirred and within minutes, he was hardly able to contain his rage.

'Go at once to the palace square,' he shouted to two of his bodyguards. 'You will see a man carrying another on his shoulders. Don't listen to any arguments or pleas but just throw down the man on the shoulders, kick him and leave him there, and bring the other man to me.' Then he withdrew from the terrace, outraged at Raman's villainy and full of sympathy for his priest.

Raman, however, had seen the king watching from

the terrace and guessed what had transpired. He sprang down from Tatachari's shoulders, caught hold of his feet and began to cry. 'Forgive me, O venerable priest!' he wailed. 'I beg your pardon for my crime. Let me carry you on *my* shoulders to atone for my mistake. But first say you forgive me, O noble one.'

Tatachari was too delighted at the change in Raman's behaviour to ponder the reason behind it. He curled his lip in disdain. 'I forgive you, Raman,' he said grandly. 'You are a thoughtless fool who is worth nothing. You can carry me as atonement and perhaps that will teach you a lesson for life—not to wrangle with your superiors.' He then seated himself on Raman's shoulders with a haughty air.

They had barely walked two steps before the burly palace guards descended on them. They knocked down the priest and gave him a choice selection of blows and kicks, completely ignoring his cries of injured protest. Then they escorted Raman to the king with great respect.

Krishna Devaraya was understandably shocked. 'Why did you bring this fellow here?' he demanded. 'I asked you to beat him up and leave him there, and bring the one who was carrying him here.'

'But we carried out your orders exactly, your majesty,' stammered the bewildered guards.

'What! Do you mean to say that this man was

carrying the other, and that you kicked the other and left him there?'

'Yes, your majesty,' they chorused.

'This man is a complete rascal!' exclaimed the king. 'Take him and bury him in a pit—and have his head trampled by an elephant.'

The irate soldiers dragged Raman away while the king hurried to appease Tatachari.

Buried neck-deep in a pit on the outskirts of the town, a very scared Raman tried to keep a cool head. The guards went off to fetch an elephant, and Raman revolved various schemes frantically in his head.

Just then a hunchbacked washerman passed by with a large bundle of clothes. He was bent over by the weight of his large hump but he stopped to stare at Raman. 'Sir, what are you doing here?' he asked.

'My good fellow, this is a special treatment,' said Raman instantly. 'It is an excellent cure for hunchbacks. I have been in this pit for an hour. Now I have to see if I'm cured. Can you help me out?'

The washerman obligingly dug Raman out of the pit. He was astounded to see the latter's straight back.

'I'm cured!' exclaimed Raman joyfully.

'Could I try it too?' asked the washerman eagerly.

'Why not?' answered Raman. 'Here, I'll help you in and I'll even deliver your clothes for you.'

The grateful washerman was soon comfortably

ensconced in the pit. Raman ran off with the bundle of clothes.

Soon after, the washerman's dreams of a perfect back were interrupted by a trumpeting sound. Opening his eyes, he was horrified to see an elephant heading straight for him.

'Help!' he screamed. 'Stop that elephant! Help!'

'That's not the jester's voice,' cried one of the guards and charged forward to stop the determined tusker.

A lengthy round of explanations followed, after which the washerman was dispatched homewards, torn between relief and anger.

Meanwhile, Krishna Devaraya's fury had abated, and in its place was a niggling doubt about whether he had been too hasty in condemning Raman to death. Tatachari's explanations seemed incomplete, as he could not satisfactorily account for Raman's hostility towards him.

As the king sat in court, he could not banish the doubt from his mind. 'If only,' he sighed aloud, 'I had Raman before me now. Then I could question him and ...'

'Your wish is granted, your majesty!' Raman came towards the king from the fringes of the crowd, throwing off a cloth with which he had cloaked his features.

Krishna Devaraya felt a mixture of emotions ranging from amusement to fury, but the predominant one was relief. And so, after hearing Raman's explanations, he threw a purse of gold towards him.

'Be careful, Raman,' he warned. 'Don't overstep your line again.'

'I won't, sir,' chirped Raman, casting a look at Tatachari that reduced that worthy priest to a state of simmering fury.

 # The Care of Horses

Krishna Devaraya was often at war with the kingdoms to the north, all of whom had a strong cavalry. The king decided that in order to be fully prepared for their attacks, his cavalry needed to be strengthened, too. Accordingly, he set about buying the finest Arabian horses that were available.

However, he was soon faced with a fresh problem. The thousand or so horses that he acquired required meticulous care. Moreover, he would need to build additional stables, which was a difficult proposition in the crowded palace grounds.

'Sir, I have a suggestion,' said the minister, Thimmarusu. 'Why don't you give the horses to selected persons with an allowance for their upkeep? You could then muster them in wartime.'

The king approved of this idea. The beautiful horses were allotted to different courtiers who were given money for grass, gram and medicine. The whole enterprise was to be supervised by the king through quarterly reviews.

Though Raman had no clue about horses and their care, he decided to ask for one, spurred by the thought of the handsome allowance involved. Stifling his misgivings, Krishna Devaraya gave in to the jester's pleas and Raman was soon the foster-owner of a strong Arabian horse with glossy skin and a splendid mane.

The beauty of this magnificent specimen was lost on Raman, however, who incarcerated the horse in a small dark shed with a little hole in the wall, at a height of about four feet from the ground. He fed it a handful of straw each day, which the wretchedly ravenous animal used to wrench from his hands. Meanwhile, the allowance was speedily exhausted on various extravagant purchases and Raman was left waiting, rather apprehensively, for the first quarterly inspection.

On the appointed day, the jester presented

himself before the king without his horse. He said rather sadly, 'I cannot bring that horse on my own. It is so impossibly fierce! Sir, please ask the master-of-horses to bring it here.'

The master-of-horses, Muhammad Anwar, a gentleman with a long, straw-coloured beard, bristled with annoyance when he heard this. 'How can it be so fierce?' he demanded. 'These horses are thoroughbreds. There is no wild streak in them.'

Raman stuck to his story, however, and invited the master-of-horses to come and see for himself. He led Muhammad Anwar to the shed near his house. 'There,' he said, pointing with a quivering finger. 'Look in through that hole. The horse is so dangerous that I was forced to shut it up in there.'

'Nonsense!' snorted the other. 'The fact is you are a coward. You don't know how to deal with horses as we soldiers do. Let me see this famous horse.'

So saying, Mohammad Anwar tried to thrust his head in through the hole. All of a sudden, he felt a sharp tug at his beard. When he tried to shake it free, he found, to his horror, that he was pinned against the outside wall of the shed. Within, the horse chewed away hungrily, mistaking the beard for his usual quota of straw.

'Help!' screamed the master-of-horses. 'Help me, Raman! The horse will not let me go!'

'I told you so!' cried Raman triumphantly and ran off to get help.

When the news reached the court, Krishna Devaraya hastened to the spot with his soldiers to see the ferocious horse for himself. Mohammad Anwar had screamed himself hoarse by then but he yelped anew when he saw the king.

'Rescue this man,' ordered an agitated Krishna Devaraya. One of the soldiers darted forward and, by dint of great caution and dexterity, sheared off the beard with a pair of scissors. The beleaguered victim fell back, nursing his sore chin with its remaining jagged tufts of hair, while the emaciated horse was led out by the other soldiers.

The king exclaimed in horror. 'What have you done to this horse, Raman?' he demanded angrily.

'Sir, despite its famished condition, the horse has done away with this officer's beard and it required the personal intervention of your majesty to save him from its clutches. I dread to think what it would have done if I had fed it properly!' was Raman's prompt reply.

The king frowned at Raman awhile. His lips, however, twitched slightly. 'You rogue! You are always ready with your smart answers. I don't want to see you in court at all.' Turning on his heel, the king strode off, instructing the master-of-horses to take personal care of the poor horse.

Two weeks passed. Raman did not dare show his face at court. Yet he could not quell a growing urge to try his luck with the king again. Surely his anger would have abated!

Accordingly, he arrived at court one evening and demanded to be let in.

'But the king said you are not to be allowed in,' protested the guard. 'And, in any case, he is watching a special dance performance and has given orders that he is not to be disturbed. I can't let you in.'

Raman shrugged his shoulders. 'Very well—but the king and I have made up recently and he particularly called me here to receive a present. He forgot to tell you, I suppose,' and he turned away.

That the king showered all sorts of presents on the jester was a commonly known fact. To the guard, this seemed like a heaven-sent opportunity. 'Wait,' he called. 'I'll let you in but you must promise to give me half of whatever the king gives you.'

Raman agreed. At the inner gate, he had a similar conversation with another guard and again promised to share half of whatever he received from the king.

Barging into the court, Raman seized a stick from one of the sentries and hit the lead dancer with it—right in the middle of a complicated dance sequence. The man howled in pain.

Krishna Devaraya, beside himself with rage at this unwelcome intrusion, shouted to the chief guard, Kama Nayaka, 'I have given too many gifts to this man and spoilt him. Now I will give him something entirely different—two dozen stripes.'

'Wait, your majesty,' said Raman quickly. 'I have already given away your gift.'

'What do you mean?' thundered the irate king.

Events unfolded rapidly, thereafter. Raman launched into an explanation, the corrupt guards were called in and given a dozen stripes each, and the king, much against his better judgement, collapsed with laughter at this unexpected episode.

'Am I forgiven then, your majesty?' Raman ventured with unusual timidity.

'You are, you rogue,' smiled the king, throwing the jester a purse of gold. 'Whatever you do, at least you make me laugh!'

Raman heaved a sigh of relief. It was nice to be back in the king's good books again!

The Famous Fruit

Tenali Raman was extremely fond of Mangamma, his wife. But this fondness did not extend towards her family, especially her brother, Pichayya.

Pichayya had turned up his nose at Raman and his grandiose plans in the beginning. Even now, when his brother-in-law was actually at court and highly regarded by the king, Pichayya's disdain had not disappeared altogether.

Raman found his brother-in-law very obnoxious and wondered at his superior attitude, considering that the latter had never stepped out of his village and knew nothing of the world outside.

However disdainful Pichayya might be, he was not averse to enjoying the luxuries of Raman's home. And since no invitation was forthcoming, he invited himself over with very little notice.

On hearing the news, Raman's face fell but he manfully strove to hide his dismay from the excited Mangamma.

'Oh, I am so happy,' sang Mangamma.

'I can well understand,' smiled the miserable Raman. 'We must treat your brother very hospitably, my dear, so that he can appreciate life as we live it— the best food and drink and so on, you know.'

Pichayya, on his arrival, was completely dazed by the town and its grandeur. His conversation with Mangamma was punctuated with cries of discovery and amazement. This pleased Raman greatly and he insisted on taking Pichayya to all the most remarkable places in Vijayanagara so as to impress him.

One day Raman offered Pichayya a wonderful array of fruits—golden mangoes, juicy custard apples, pineapples, papayas and cashews. Pichayya stuffed his mouth with these delicacies and closed his eyes in ecstasy. 'This is nectar,' he murmured and happily stuffed his mouth again and again till the plate was empty.

'Where did you get these delicious fruits?' he asked. 'I want to have more.'

'These are from the king's garden,' replied Raman. 'The Sultan of Bijapur gifted ten plants of these special grafted mangoes from his own palace orchard to the king, while the Portuguese brought the other fruits. All the fruits belong to the king alone and are found only in his garden. He is very possessive about them and has warned that anyone caught stealing them will get the death penalty.'

'How did you get them then?' demanded Pichayya.

Raman smirked. 'I enjoy the favour of the king. So he keeps giving me special things.'

Pichayya stared at him with barely-concealed jealousy in his eye. And, right then, an obstinate resolve formed in his head. He would steal some fruits from the royal garden and have his fill of them. 'Who will miss a few fruits from this garden?' he thought to himself.

That night, after Raman and Mangamma had fallen asleep, Pichayya crept out of the house and made his way to the palace. He had already been taken on several tours near it, so he remembered the way very well. He managed to slip noiselessly into the garden, aided by the fact that it was a moonless night and pitch dark all around.

As his eyes grew accustomed to the dark, he saw an amazing variety of fruit hanging before him in luscious bunches. Plucking and stuffing them into his mouth was, for him, the work of a moment. As the delicious juices trickled down his chin, he gave grunts of satisfaction. These grunts soon grew to loud appreciation.

'Wonderful!' exclaimed Pichayya as the last of a mango disappeared down his throat. 'Excellent!' he cried as he bit into a custard apple. 'Magnificent!' he observed as he seized a large papaya.

At that very moment, he saw a grim-faced sentry making his way towards him.

Too late, Pichayya realised the pitfalls of being a noisy thief. In vain, he protested that he was Raman's brother-in-law. He spent the rest of the night in jail unhappily contemplating his excesses and wondering what the morrow would bring.

The following day, an enraged Krishna Devaraya summarily announced Pichayya's execution. If the man had dared to help himself to those precious fruits, then he must pay for it!

Raman and Mangamma were wondering where Pichayya was when the news reached them. Mangamma wailed and wrung her hands in despair. 'You must save my brother,' she begged Raman. 'You must somehow do it.'

'I don't know,' said Raman gloomily. 'I told him that the king was touchy about the fruits, didn't I? Then what made him ...?'

'I don't want to hear anything,' broke in Mangamma. 'You alone can save him. Do it for my sake.'

'All right,' said Raman heavily. 'But don't be too hopeful.' He made his way to the court, full of trepidation.

Krishna Devaraya took one look at Raman and said, 'I know why you have come. But I swear I will not do what you are about to ask me about your brother-in-law.'

'I ask you to put the greedy rascal to death,' said Raman promptly.

The king was astounded. 'What ...?'

Raman continued, 'And remember, sir, you have sworn not to do what I ask you to do about him.'

The king was speechless for a moment. Then he threw back his head, laughing heartily. 'Raman, you have cornered me,' he declared. 'I can't hang that rogue now. But see that he leaves the town at once.'

'I shall do so for my own sake,' replied Raman, breathing a sigh of relief.

Pichayya was duly released and delivered into the loving hands of his sister. However, his near brush with death had so terrified him that he refused to stay a minute longer than necessary. He packed his belongings and was out of the house within an hour of his release, his sister's protestations notwithstanding. Raman hoped that he had seen the last of his brother-in-law—for some time at least!

The Art of the Painter

One day, Krishna Devaraya took his ministers and courtiers to a new palace that he had built some distance away from the old one.

A celebrated artist had executed some fine paintings on the palace walls and the king was anxious for the others to admire them. 'Aren't they beautiful?' he murmured, staring at the lifelike scenes from the *Ramayana* and the *Mahabharata*. There was a chorus of assent but Raman looked distinctly perplexed.

'There's something I don't understand,' he piped

up, jabbing his finger at a painting of the epic hero, Rama, in profile. 'Where is the other half of the face?'

'That is a profile, you fool,' laughed the king. 'You have to imagine the other half. Isn't that obvious?'

The others sniggered at Rama's ignorance, which made him bristle with annoyance. However, he made no other comment and the issue was dropped.

A month later, Raman informed the king that he had been learning to paint. 'I can excel all the paintings you've seen,' he boasted. 'I think I have perfected the art.'

'That is wonderful,' said the king. 'Wait, I'll give you a chance to prove your talent. You can paint on the walls of the summer palace—but have it ready as soon as possible, for I am expecting a honoured guest shortly who will stay there.'

Raman plunged into his work with a will. A month later, he invited the king and the courtiers to see his handiwork.

When the courtiers assembled at the summer palace, there was initially a strained silence among the group.

An indignant Krishna Devaraya broke the hush. 'What have you done to the walls, Raman?' he stormed. 'You have drawn bits of the body everywhere—arms, legs, knees, elbows, shoulders, noses, ears, teeth ...! What is this nonsense? Where are the other parts of the body?'

'You have to imagine them, of course,' observed Raman smoothly. 'Isn't that obvious, sir?'

The king was so angry that he could not speak for a few moments. Then he exploded. 'You fool! You have ruined the walls of this palace! How will I get them ready in time for my guest?'

Swivelling around, he caught sight of two sentries and called them. 'I am sick of this fellow,' he shouted. 'Take him away and cut off his head with one sweep of your swords.'

Raman was dragged off unceremoniously, while the king stared in dismay at the disfigured walls.

'I have one last request,' Raman told the sentries as they led him away. 'I want to pray to God, standing waist-deep in water for an hour, before you kill me. That way I might just be able to go to heaven.'

'All right,' said one sentry. 'But you better not try any of your tricks.'

'I won't,' Raman shook his head vehemently. 'You stand by me with drawn swords and cut off my neck if I try to escape.'

The three men reached the river and waded out into it. While Raman muttered his prayers with his eyes shut, the sentries stood on either side of him, ready to strike if he made a bid for freedom. A short while later, the two sentries began to feel distinctly uncomfortable with the cold water swirling around their legs, and their clothes wet and heavy. Yet they did not feel like disturbing the devout man, especially since he was condemned to die shortly.

After about three quarters of an hour, Raman suddenly cried out, 'Cut!' and dived into the water. The confused sentries lashed out with their swords but metal clanged uselessly on metal. Raman was nowhere in sight.

Splashing wildly about, they finally managed to locate the soaked jester and haul him to the bank.

As they raised their swords to kill him, Raman shouted, 'Wait! You are disobeying the king's orders.'

'What do you mean?' roared the sentries.

'Just that,' smiled Raman. 'He ordered you to cut off my head with one sweep of your swords but you failed. He didn't say anything about a second attempt. So now you cannot kill me.'

The guards had nothing to say to this. The trio trudged back to the palace in silence, dripping water with every step.

Knowing Krishna Devaraya, Raman suspected that the king's fury would have abated and he would be starting to feel remorseful. So he entered the court boldly, saying, 'Sir, a human life is worth much more than damaged walls.'

The king jumped up in surprise and relief. 'How did you escape?'

Raman told him the story and, in no time at all, the king was convulsed with laughter.

'You are impossibly shrewd, Raman,' he said at last. 'I forgive you this time as I admire your presence of mind and your courage. But don't play any other silly pranks in future.'

'Oh no, I won't, sir,' was the fervent reply. And a relieved Raman ran home to change his clothes.

The One Who Never Yawned

As with most kings, Krishna Devaraya had several queens. Queen Tirumaladevi was the one that Raman liked most. She was witty and had a great sense of humour that made her appreciate Raman's witticisms and jests all the more.

When she sent for him one day, Raman assumed that she wanted to be regaled with jokes and funny stories as usual. To his dismay, however, he found the queen was very upset.

'What is the matter?' he asked, deeply concerned.

'The king is angry with me,' she replied. 'And it wasn't really my fault. You have got to help me.'

'I will,' assured Raman. 'But tell me the whole story first.'

Queen Tirumaladevi sighed. 'The king was reading his latest play to me. It's called *Jambavati Kalyanam*. I was listening carefully when suddenly, I felt an urge to yawn. I tried to stifle it but couldn't help it after a while. And so I yawned.' She paused and sighed again. 'The king was furious. He just walked off with the play and I haven't seen him since.'

'The matter is simple then,' exclaimed a relieved Raman. 'All you have to do is apologise.'

'Don't be silly, Raman,' snapped the queen. 'Of course I've apologised but it had absolutely no effect.' She looked thoughtful for a while and then said slowly. 'When the king was angry with Queen Chinnadevi because she slept with her feet on his portrait carved on her bedstead, she got the poet Nandi Thimmana to write a poem on how love makes us take liberties. And so he forgave her immediately. Now *you* have to help me.'

'I cannot write a poem on yawning,' retorted Raman with asperity. 'But I shall resolve the matter in my own way.'

Raman left, thinking furiously. Soon an idea slid into his head.

The following day at court, the discussion was about the rice situation in the ceded districts of the Vijayanagara empire. This had been slated beforehand and so, Raman sat waiting for his cue.

'We must increase the rice production in these areas,' observed the king. 'But how do we do it? We've provided water through the Raya channel and the Nagalapuram tank—but clearly this is not enough.'

Raman promptly jumped to his feet, waving a paddy seed in his hand. 'I have the solution here, your majesty. If this particular seed is used, the yield will increase to thrice the present one.'

'That's wonderful!' said the king enthusiastically. 'This will solve all our problems. But where did you get this special seed? Does it require special soil or manure or ...?'

'Oh no, nothing like that,' replied Raman. 'The only requirement is that it be sown, and the crop reared and reaped by one who has never yawned in his life and never will.'

'You idiot!' exclaimed the king. 'Is there a single person in the whole world who has never yawned? Can anyone ever stop themselves from yawning?'

'I forgot that,' observed Raman ruefully. 'How foolish of me! I'm glad you reminded me, sir. I must go and tell Queen Tirumaladevi about this folly of mine.'

There was silence for a moment. The king seemed on the verge of losing his temper but then looked very thoughtful. After a few moments, he smiled at Raman. 'No, wait. I will go and tell her myself.' He threw a purse of gold at Raman. 'You deserve this,' he said and went to make up with the queen.

A short while later, Raman was in possession of another purse of gold—and this one was from the grateful queen.

A Bee in the Royal Bonnet

There were many things that Raman liked about Krishna Devaraya—his genorosity, sense of humour and intelligence, for instance. However, there were several equally annoying aspects to the king's character, among them being his fetish for cleanliness. There was, of course, nothing wrong in being concerned about cleanliness but the king was capable of carrying it to extraordinary limits.

Raman got a taste of this when he was strolling about with the king one morning. Engrossed in a discussion, he didn't quite notice where he was going and trod on some dirt lying on the edge of the road.

Raman stared in distaste at the small toe of his right foot that was now brown and filthy where the dirt had oozed over. Fortunately, there was a channel nearby and the jester cleaned his foot there, scrubbing the toe well with earth and water.

When Raman rejoined the king, the latter wrinkled his nose in a fastidious fashion. 'However much you wash it, some amount of dirt will stick to your toe. So the only way to get rid of it is to cut that little toe off,' he observed calmly.

Raman gaped in surprise. 'But you saw me scrub the toe with earth and wash it several times with water,' he protested.

The king waved his hand dismissively. 'That would only have driven some of the filth in. Don't enter my private room or your horrible toe will ruin my lovely Persian carpets.'

Raman was thoroughly annoyed. He said, a little sharply, 'What if I convince you that you are wrong, sir?'

'Try if you want,' the king shrugged his shoulders, 'but I am definitely not going to change my opinion.'

An extremely vexed Raman vended his way homewards, thinking hard of a suitable plan. And as his ideas began to come, his irritation melted away like magic.

Raman stayed away from court for a few days. He was, however, very busy for he bought some fine rose plants and planted them in a pit full of filth in his garden. He covered the muck with a light layer of turf and stood back, very pleased with the result of his labours.

A few days later, when the roses were in full bloom, Raman waylaid the king on his daily walk and begged him to inspect the flowers. 'They are so beautiful,' he murmured persuasively. 'A lover of nature like you should not miss this chance of seeing them in full glory.'

'I'd love to see them,' the king smiled. 'Come, let's go to your house right away.'

When the king caught sight of the roses, he was unstinted in his praise. 'What lovely roses!' he cried. ' I must go closer and see them properly.'

So saying, he stepped on to the turf. The thin layer promptly gave way and the king sank up to his neck in the filth of the pit.

Ignoring the king's cry of alarm, Raman shouted, 'Wait a minute. Let me bring a sword and cut off the dirty portion neatly at the neck.'

The king gaped at his jester. 'What? Do you want to cut my head off?' he stuttered when he could finally find his voice.

Raman nodded emphatically. 'What else can be

done? You told me the other day that I would be clean only if I cut off my toe. So a similar treatment will cleanse your body, too.' He paused. 'Or have you, by any chance, revised your opinion?'

Krishna Devaraya ground his teeth in frustration. 'Yes, yes—I've revised my opinion,' he barked. 'Now pull me out of here quickly before anyone else sees me in this state.'

Raman's eyes gleamed with triumph as he pulled the king out of the messy pit. That was the end of one foolish fetish at least!

The Bundle of Wisdom

Krishna Devaraya's patronage of talented people was legendary. The Vijayanagara court had a formidable reputation in the realm of learning and the arts. It was said that the *ashtadiggajas* or 'the eight elephants of learning' at this court, of whom Raman was one, could defeat anybody in debates or in tests of literary talent.

It was, therefore, inevitable that Rama Sastri, a celebrated scholar from Bengal, would want to prove himself in the Vijayanagara court. He had recently enjoyed scholarly triumphs at the courts of Varanasi and Orissa, and after this he hastened to the Vijayanagara court and challenged the scholars there to a contest.

Krishna Devaraya smiled benignly at the great scholar's offer. He was confident that one of his eight gems would rise to the challenge, trounce this arrogant visitor in learning and argument, and retain the honour of his court. But, to his great dismay, once Rama Sastri had left the court after issuing his challenge, he realised that none of them dared pick up the gauntlet. When his taunts and threats proved to be futile, the king resorted to individual appeals but even these bore no fruit.

'Why are you so scared?' demanded the frustrated king.

'Rama Sastri's formidable reputation makes the best of debaters scurry away,' said the poet, Allasani Peddanna, grimly. 'What is the point in pitting our skills against his?'

Thimmanna, Ramabhadriah and the others nodded fervently. The king tried to coax, wheedle and command anew, but even these failed to move the stalwarts. Krishna Devaraya took a final look at his mutinous court scholars and sighed. 'All right then,' he muttered. 'We have no option but to acknowledge defeat.'

Raman had been silent all this while. Now he

murmured, 'No, sir, not while I am here.'

The king turned to him, a desperate plea in his eye, 'What can *you* do against this scholar, Raman?'

'Well,' began Raman in injured tones, 'everyone keeps forgetting that I am the author of two great works—the *Panduranga Mahatmya* and the *Lingapurana*. In any case, I can definitely pit my commonsense against his bookish learning and defeat him.'

'How?' snapped the king, looking a trifle sceptical.

'Just let these worthy gentlemen help me,' said Raman, gesturing towards the silent scholars, 'and I will do the needful.'

'All right,' said the king, reflecting somewhat uneasily on Raman's penchant for pranks and wondering what he had in mind.

The following morning, Raman entered the court with great fanfare. Dressed in his best clothes and surrounded by the other court scholars, he strode forward, his head high, and cradling a big booklike bundle wrapped in fine silk in his arms. Krishna Devaraya raised his eyebrows at this intriguing sight but forbore from asking any questions.

Rama Sastri bowed low before Raman—who responded likewise—and then, unable to contain his curiosity, asked, 'Could you tell me what that book is?'

'This?' Raman gestured towards his bundle. 'Oh, it is only *Tilakashta-mahisha-bandhanam*—my new book that deals with anagrams and related matters.'

The great scholar took a step backwards and blinked. He searched his memory frantically but could not recall having heard of this book or its contents.

'We will begin the discussion tomorrow with this book,' continued Raman. 'Then we can move on to more complex ones.' He stifled a yawn and looked around with a bored expression.

The significance of Raman's tone and gestures was not lost on Rama Sastri. He managed to stammer his assent and went back to his lodgings as soon as he could. Feeling thoroughly confused and apprehensive, he pondered deep and hard over the obstacles that had suddenly sprung up in his path. In the first place, he would have to debate over an unknown book of voluminous proportions. And then his opponent seemed such a mighty scholar that the others danced attendance on him and he himself evidently regarded the challenge as an uninteresting, run-of-the-mill affair. Perhaps he was used to routing scholars with such ease that the very thought of a debate failed to excite him any more.

Rama Sastri stood among his treatises, his mind whirling with doubt. 'I better run away from here,' he resolved at last. 'I am sure to lose the debate and then my reputation will be shattered.'

And so, a craven figure fled the city that night—a stark contrast to the supercilious man who had entered it only two days earlier.

The king and the court learned of Rama Sastri's departure when he did not turn up for the debate the following day. Raman preened and smirked while the other scholars heaved gusty sighs of relief.

'Well, that's a funny end to the challenge,' mused the king. 'But, Raman—show us this formidable book that achieved your victory.'

Raman promptly whisked off the silk covering. The bundle contained a number of twigs of the sesamum plant, tied up with a rope commonly used to tether buffaloes.

Krishna Devaraya gaped at it. 'What is this?' he demanded.

'I told you all what it was,' said the jester in aggrieved tones. 'It is *tilakashta*—or sesamum twigs—tied up with buffalo rope—or *mahisha bandhanam*. That's the exact truth, isn't it?'

The king whooped with laughter, as did the other scholars. Raman was given a purse of gold for preserving the honour of the Vijayanagara court.

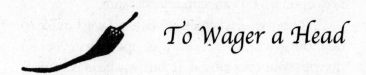

To Wager a Head

There was great excitement at the court of Vijayanagara. A famous magician from the north was visiting, and his audience clapped and cheered as he made pebbles turn into gold coins, produced perfumes of varied kinds from thin air, and even cut off his head and held it in his hands. Krishna Devaraya was deeply impressed and expressed his praise in no uncertain terms.

Emboldened, the magician declared, 'I have no rival in this country, O king. I am clearly the best. So

I challenge anyone here to any trick or feat and if I lose, I forfeit my head to the victor.'

The king frowned. He disliked having any outsider claim superiority over his people. When the magician departed, he called Raman and said, 'I'll give you a thousand gold coins if you accept this man's challenge and defeat him. Can you do this for me?'

'Of course,' was Raman's prompt answer.

That very day, he tracked down the magician and told him, 'I'm quite sure you cannot do with your eyes open what I can with my eyes shut.'

'Nonsense!' exclaimed the latter. 'I will be able to do more gracefully with my eyes open whatever you do with your eyes closed. If not, my head is yours.'

The two made their way back to the court where the challenge was proclaimed. The king and the courtiers gathered to watch with great interest.

Raman produced a container of chilli powder from his pocket with a flourish. He shut his eyes firmly and put a tablespoonful of the powder over each of his eyelids. For a whole minute he stood there, balancing the powder on his eyelids and smiling the while. At the end of the minute, he removed the powder carefully, washed his eyelids thoroughly and looked at the stunned magician.

'All right, now it's your turn. Do what I did gracefully with your eyes open—or pay the forfeit.'

The magician swallowed hard and looked around desperately for a solution. Finally, he threw up his hands in defeat. 'I give up. I cannot do what you ask of me. So my head is yours now.'

Raman shrugged his shoulders and laughed. 'What will I do with your head? I have no use for it—and, in any case, I am quite satisfied with my victory.'

The magician beat a hasty retreat from the court while an overjoyed Krishna Devaraya gave the prize money to his clever jester. Raman almost danced the entire way home and spent the rest of the day gloating over his victory.

Danger in the Garden

The governor of South Kanara, knowing of the king's love for good food, had gifted Krishna Devaraya some brinjal plants. The brinjal from these plants, he said, could be made into a magnificent curry.

When the plants eventually bore fruit and the king got to taste the brinjal curry, he was ecstatic. 'What a divine dish!' he exclaimed in joy.

Raman happened to be with the king, and he was offered a bit of the curry. He too had to agree with the king that the flavours were exquisite.

At home that evening, Raman was almost lyrical in his praise of the curry. This made Mangamma envious. 'I must taste these brinjals too,' she declared. 'You have to get them for me.'

'I can't,' said Raman flatly. 'The king guards them jealously and will behead anyone caught stealing them. Don't you remember Pichayya's experience?'

Mangamma's face took on a mulish look. 'Don't compare yourself with Pichayya. And, in any case, I've never asked you yet for any favour. So you just have to fulfil my request.'

Raman looked troubled. 'It's a huge risk.'

Mangamma's head was swirling with visions of delicious curry and she didn't care, at the moment, for anything else. Normally a mild and contented soul, she could be amazingly obstinate and unreasonable when she chose.

'Just do it for me,' she said and turned away.

Raman wondered whether to list all the risks involved but abandoned the idea after recognising the look on her face.

The following night, Raman crept into the king's garden and deftly picked a dozen fine brinjals under the cover of darkness. As he was tiptoeing out, his heart gave an unpleasant lurch, for in front of him—though some distance away—loomed the unmistakeable form of Appaji, the prime minister.

It would never do for Appaji to catch him—for he had been at the receiving end of Raman's pranks many a time and cordially detested the jester. Raman ducked behind a convenient bush and later fled back home, unobserved and triumphant.

Mangamma seized the brinjals joyfully and proceeded to make the curry. Soon delectable smells were wafting around the house and Raman wiggled his nose in delight.

As she ate the first mouthful of the curry, Mangamma shut her eyes in bliss. 'This is the best curry I've ever tasted!' she exclaimed, smacking her lips in delight. 'What flavours! What aromas!'

Raman nodded as he shovelled some into his mouth.

However, just then, Mangamma put an effective stop to his enjoyment. 'We've got to give some to our son too,' she declared.

Raman's appetite waned instantly. He shook his head vigorously. 'Don't be foolish! Gopa is only six years old and if he's questioned, he'll babble the truth. We can't take the risk—we'll be ruined. Is that what you want?'

'I don't care,' said Mangamma stubbornly, sticking out her lower lip and folding her arms in a gesture that Raman knew all too well. It meant that the normally gentle Mangamma would not be moved.

'I'm a mother and I can't deprive my son of such a treat. So you better think of some way in which he can eat the curry and yet not get us into trouble.'

Raman sighed. 'All right,' he said.

Little Gopa was sleeping outside on the terrace, as it was a hot summer night. Raman took a pot of water and emptied the contents over his son, soaking him completely. The boy woke up in shock.

'It is raining,' said his father solicitously. 'Come in, change your clothes and eat what your mother has cooked.'

While the sleepy child's clothes were being changed, Mangamma fed him the curry which he ate with great enjoyment, smacking his lips and sighing.

'Now sleep inside the house,' ordered Raman. 'It's raining hard outside.'

The following morning, there was an outcry at the court because of the missing brinjals. The king paced up and down, his face purple and his fists clenched.

'Just find the thief,' he shouted to the guards around him. 'The one who brings the rogue to me will get a huge reward.'

At that moment, something clicked in Appaji's mind and he stepped forward. 'Sir, I saw Raman near the garden last night. But he vanished quite suddenly and I couldn't find him later.'

Krishna Devaraya stopped in mid-stride, his face suddenly thoughtful. 'Yes, this is exactly the sort of daring prank Raman would play,' he said slowly. 'But how do we get him to admit it?' The thought of his beloved brinjals smote him with a fresh stab of pain and he snapped his fingers. 'Get Raman's son here. He will tell us the truth.'

And so, Gopa was produced in court and he faced the king with startling composure—almost like his father, thought Appaji bitterly. He caught Raman's eye, smiled a triumphant smile and stepped forward, at his threatening best.

'What curry did you have last night, boy?' Appaji asked grimly.

'A wonderful brinjal curry,' replied Gopa stoutly.

'Your theft is proved now,' Appaji told Raman. 'Own up—if you dare.'

'Nonsense!' said Raman calmly and spread out his hands. 'My son was fast asleep all night and is clearly talking about his dreams. He must have overheard me discussing with my wife the curry I shared with the king—and then he dreamed about it. Let me make things even clearer. Ask him whether last night was rainy or clear.'

'Boy, was it raining last night or was it clear?' boomed Appaji.

Gopa piped up, 'It rained very hard. I got

completely wet and had to change my clothes.'

Appaji looked bewildered and so did everyone else. There had not been a drop of rain the previous night. The prime minister coughed, cleared his throat and shuffled his feet. Then, when he was unable to put off the moment any longer, he turned to Raman and muttered a hasty apology for the unjust accusation.

Raman waved his hand magnanimously. 'Forget it. People make mistakes all the time.'

A while later, father and son made their way homewards, discussing the weirdness of Appaji and the merits of brinjal curry.

The Snake in the Grass

Krishna Devaraya was not only famous as a patron of art and literature, he was also regarded as a formidable fighter and military strategist. It was this that gave the Sultan of Bijapur many a sleepless night. He knew that Krishna Devaraya was preparing to attack him (as well as the kings of Raichur and Gulbarga), and he needed desperate measures to face such a mighty enemy.

The Sultan summoned his cleverest spy, a Muslim called Raja Sahib. 'Go at once to Vijayanagara,' he said. 'Disguise yourself as a Tamil brahmana—that should not be a problem since you are dark and, more importantly, you know all the rites, customs and manners of that community. Worm yourself into Krishna Devaraya's confidence and kill him at a suitable opportunity. Then I will not have to fear being invaded by him and perhaps *I* can invade Vijayanagara in the confusion following his death.'

Raja Sahib set out on his mission with alacrity. He was fiercely loyal to his Sultan but he also had a personal grudge against the Vijayanagara rulers. He was descended from the Sultans of Madura who had been uprooted by the Vijayanagara emperors.

Assuming the name Raja Aiyar and dressed in appropriate clothes, Raja Sahib entered the Vijayanagara court and presented himself to the king. In no time at all, Krishna Devaraya was impressed by this smooth-talking Tamil brahmana and his wide knowledge of the *Vedas*, *Sastras* and *Puranas*, from which he frequently quoted.

To Raman, however, it seemed that there was something a little too perfect about this visitor. His answers were too pat and his knowledge too precise—and this set him thinking.

In a matter of a few days, Raja Sahib had thoroughly ingratiated himself with the king and received many generous presents from him. Moreover, he was even given permission to visit the palace at any time of the day or night—a privilege extended only to very favoured persons. Raja Sahib was thrilled at this initial success but he knew that he had to proceed cautiously.

He took a couple of weeks to familiarise himself with the inner apartments of the palace, looking for a perfect place from which he could attack the king. But he also realised that there were two major problems he had to solve. The first was that there were always a large number of men who thronged around the popular king, laughing and exchanging jokes all the while. It was on very rare occasions that the king could be found alone, and unless he was alone any attack would be swiftly overpowered.

The second problem was Raman. It seemed to Raja Sahib that Raman's eyes were always on him, appraising him in a cool manner that made the spy distinctly uncomfortable. Besides, Raman seemed to stick like a leech to the king. So what was an aspiring assassin to do in these circumstances? Nothing, reflected Raja Sahib bitterly, except bide one's time and take one's chances.

Meanwhile, Raman's suspicions were growing by the day. He began to bait Raja Sahib in court, testing his knowledge of the scriptures and smoothly inserting ambiguous remarks in the conversation to gauge the latter's reactions.

After a particularly hostile verbal duel, the king felt the need to remonstrate with his jester. 'You talk to Raja Aiyar in a very peculiar manner, Raman. Why do you dislike him so?'

'Because,' said Raman bluntly, 'I have a feeling he is a spy of one of the Sultans. And his knowledge of the scriptures is so perfect that I think he is not a brahmana. You are creating problems for yourself by favouring him time and again.'

'Are you crazy?' demanded the king. 'He is a pure Tamil brahmana and a truly pious man. His Sanskrit is grammatically purer than yours and he performs religious rites more punctiliously than you do.'

'That doesn't prove anything,' countered Raman. 'A foreigner will speak more grammatically than a native. And a pretender will perform ceremonies more painstakingly than a true follower.'

Krishna Devaraya still looked disbelieving. 'Why would the Sultans want to harm me—presuming he is their spy?' he asked. 'After all, even if I die, all my men remain.'

'The value is in the worth, not in the numbers,' said Raman dryly. 'You alone are equal to a million men. And without you, your army will crumble and the enemy will destroy us. Now can you see that he is a spy? Will you let me expose him?'

The king looked extremely thoughtful. 'There is

something in what you say. But how will you prove it?'

'Trust me,' said Raman briskly. 'I will unmask this villain by a simple experiment. After all,' he added mysteriously, 'what is bred in the bone will stick to the flesh.'

'I give you permission,' said the king, still struggling with some lingering doubts, 'but I want to be there while you do it—and you mustn't harm him in any way.'

Raman agreed and fixed that night for the execution of the plan. And so, while the rest of the palace slept, Raman and the king crept into Raja Sahib's room.

The jester walked up to the sleeping spy and emptied a pot of ice-cold water on his head. Raja Sahib shrieked and sprang up, shouting, 'Allah! Allah! Din! Din!' and brandished his sword at Raman. The king, temporarily stupefied by the scene, recollected himself in time and jumped into the fray, cutting off the spy's head with his sword.

Shuddering at his narrow escape, Krishna Devaraya thanked Raman profusely for saving his life and for reminding him that a king should not trust foreigners easily. And, of course, Raman took home his usual purse of gold. This time, though, the contents were doubled.

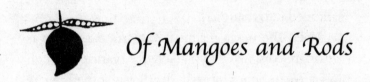

Of Mangoes and Rods

Krishna Devaraya was extremely fond of his mother. When she died, he was practically inconsolable. His grief at her death was compounded by the fact that she had wanted to eat a mango but died before it could be brought to her. 'I couldn't fulfil my mother's last wish,' he mourned. 'If only she had been able to eat that mango!'

Feeling increasingly disturbed and restless, the king consulted Tatachari, the old priest, on the matter. 'What should I do to appease my mother's spirit?' he asked.

Tatachari's eyes gleamed. Here was a wonderful opportunity for him and his fraternity to gain some riches. 'It is very simple, sir,' he informed the king. 'If a person dies without getting what he wanted, then his soul will be satisfied if the same thing is given to the priests. Give a 108 priests a gold mango each and your mother's spirit will be satisfied.'

The king, feeling immensely relieved, gave orders for large quantities of gold to be procured and fashioned into mangoes.

When the news reached Raman's ears, he was thoroughly disgusted by Tatachari's avarice. Though not averse to riches himself, death was something he considered sacred and the fact that it was being used to extract riches in this blatant manner annoyed him greatly. So while the 108 beneficiaries went home with their gold mangoes, Raman was busy making arrangements of another kind.

After a week, Raman went to Tatachari and said, with lowered eyes and humble mien, 'I have a favour to ask of you.'

Tatachari's hostility towards the jester had not lessened in any manner. Thus, he raised his eyebrows and snapped, 'What is it?'

'It is to do with my mother's death,' mumbled Raman. 'I could not fulfil her last wish and I feel terrible about that. I was told that if the same thing is given to the priests, then her soul will be appeased. So will you come to my house tomorrow—with as many priests as you can get—to accept my mother's last wish on her behalf?'

Tatachari's nose scented another heaven-sent opportunity for making money. Raman was supposed to be extremely rich—what with the numerous purses of gold and other costly presents that he regularly received from the king.

Aloud he said, 'Of course, Raman. I will bring some priests to your house tomorrow and you can make the offering.'

Raman thanked him profusely and sped on homewards.

The following day, Tatachari rounded up the other 107 priests and led them to Raman's house. The priests could hardly restrain themselves from rubbing their hands in glee. Dreaming of the fabulous presents they would get, they filed into Raman's house. They hardly noticed that the doors were securely locked behind them as soon as they entered, and that men bearing red-hot irons surrounded them.

Raman clapped his hands to get the attention of the jostling throng and said, 'Let the branding begin.'

At first, the priests eyed him in silent stupefaction. Then there was a cacophony of shrieks and screams as Raman's men began to brand them with the irons. Some of the priests wriggled out of their captors' grasp, rushed wildly to the doors and managed to escape, Tatachari being among the lucky ones.

Racing to the court, Tatachari burst in angrily upon the king and choked out an account of the outrage.

'Bring that rascal here and rescue those priests,' ordered the king. Raman had gone too far this time, decided Krishna Devaraya, furious at this latest atrocious prank. He awaited Raman's arrival impatiently, his rage growing with every passing moment.

By the time the jester arrived, he was so angry that he could barely demand an explanation.

Raman spread out his hands and looked at the king with wide-eyed innocence. 'I don't know what all the fuss is about. My mother died of rheumatism and her last wish was to be branded so as to lessen the pain. She died before I could heat the irons and I felt bad that I couldn't fulfil her wish. Then I was told that if one gave what a dying person wanted but couldn't get in time, to the priests, then the soul would be appeased.' He cast a look at Tatachari, at this juncture, and added in injured tones, 'And, in fact, Tatachari agreed to accept the offerings on my mother's behalf to satisfy her soul. Now when I am fulfilling her last wish and branding them, they are complaining.' There was a distinctly querulous note in his voice by the end of this statement as he looked plaintively at Tatachari.

Tatachari did not meet his eye but stood staring fixedly at the floor as if fascinated by it. The king, too, looked very pensive. He said, 'Tatachari, I would like to speak to you—and all those other priests as well.'

Tatachari shuffled forward unhappily while Raman cleared his throat in an exaggerated fashion and prepared to leave the two parties together. He had made his point, after all!

The Bridal Shoe

Krishna Devaraya and Raman would have discussions on any and every subject and both enjoyed these sessions a great deal. However, the king was apt to be rather mulish in his stance and Raman could not help being irritated by his attitude at times.

One such instance came about while they were discussing how gullible people could be. The king remarked, 'I don't believe that anyone can be wholly credulous. You can't fool people so easily.'

'I don't agree,' retorted Raman. 'I can make

anyone believe or do what I want them to.'

The king snorted disbelievingly and this annoyed Raman greatly. 'Why,' he continued, 'I can even make a person throw a shoe at you in the belief that he is doing the right thing.'

'Oh, really?' laughed the king. 'I challenge you to do that.'

'I accept the challenge,' said Raman at once. 'But I need some time.'

'Take as long as you like,' said the king, and promptly forgot all about the argument.

A month later, there was great excitement at the Vijayanagara court. The king was to marry Sharadambal, the beautiful daughter of a hill chieftain in Coorg. The chieftain was extremely nervous because he had no idea of the ceremonies and rites to be performed or of what was expected of him on the occasion. He tentatively voiced his doubts to the king who merely remarked, 'I'm not particular about the ceremonies since customs vary from place to place. I am only interested in your daughter.'

This was not a particularly helpful statement. The chieftain was still on tenterhooks until the day Raman paid a secret visit to Coorg and sought an audience with him. In no time at all, he had poured out all his worries to the sympathetic jester.

'Your worries are over,' said Raman soothingly.

'I'll tell you what is expected of you but you must promise not to tell anyone that I coached you. Let it be a wonderful surprise for the king.'

The chieftain swore himself to secrecy and listened attentively to Raman's instructions. At the end, Raman said, 'There is a very important rite that needs to be performed. The bride should wear a velvet shoe and throw it at her husband after the wedding ceremony, when he is about to take her home. In fact, I have even bought a beautiful pair of the traditional shoes used for this purpose.'

The chieftain looked uncertain. 'But how can a wife throw shoes at her husband? It is an improper act.'

'Not in this family,' said Raman reassuringly. 'In fact, even Europeans follow the custom but they use leather shoes instead of velvet. Of course,' he hesitated, 'if you don't want your daughter to do what princesses of the blood do, then forget about the whole thing.'

The chieftain flushed with annoyance. 'My daughter is no inferior to any other princess,' he said firmly. 'Give me the shoes and I will see that the custom is observed.'

Shortly thereafter, the wedding was celebrated with great pomp and festivity. The bride and groom looked radiantly happy together. Then, just as they were about to depart for Vijayanagara, Sharadambal took off one of her velvet shoes and threw it at Krishna Devaraya, her face aglow with happiness but with a tiny frown wrinkling her brow. The king ducked sharply, rubbing his cheek where the shoe had grazed it, and stared, thunderstruck, at his bride. The crowd was equally mystified and aghast.

Just then Raman whispered to the king, 'It's not her fault. I told her to do it. You must forgive her.'

Meanwhile, Sharadambal rushed up to her husband, begging his pardon for hitting him and asking anxiously if he were hurt. The king made a strangled noise, shook his head and then handed the shoe back to his bride, a weak smile on his face.

Once back at Vijayanagara, he got the whole story out of Raman and said grimly, 'Yes, you have won the challenge. Some people *can* be extremely credulous. But I am simply furious with you for using this outrageous way to prove it. Don't show your face at the court tomorrow or else I'll have you whipped!' He strode away, leaving Raman staring after him and wondering how to tackle this latest complication.

The following morning, Krishna Devaraya heard an uproar in the main hall even as he was approaching it. Wondering at the tumult, he walked in to find everyone clustered around Raman who wore a huge, decorated mud pot over his head that completely covered his face.

'I warned you, didn't I?' began the belligerent king. 'Now I'll have you whipped for disobeying my orders and ...'

'What?' broke in Raman in a muffled tone. 'But I have obeyed your orders exactly, sir. You told me not to show my face at court—and I haven't. All of it is hidden by this pot, isn't it?'

The king stared at him exasperatedly and then his shoulders shook. For a while, nothing could be heard except the king's guffaws. Raman felt encouraged enough to remove the cumbersome pot from his head.

'Oh, Raman!' the king said at last, wiping away tears of mirth. 'It is just no use getting angry with you!'

Raman grinned back at him and nodded. 'No use at all, sir,' he said.

Well Water and Hot Water

When a drought descended on Vijayanagara and its neighbouring areas one year, it caught everyone unawares. Water suddenly became a very precious commodity and frantic attempts were made by the king and his court to resolve the problem.

When matters were limping back to normal, a fresh problem arose in the city. A gang of robbers began to strike terror into the hearts of the citizens by their daring raids.

They seemed to be able to strike merrily at will and make away with huge amounts of money and jewellery, while miraculously eluding the guards.

The king grew increasingly short-tempered as there was episode after episode of burglary. Meanwhile, the rains were still delayed and no one knew when the drought problem would resurface.

One evening as Raman was returning home from court, mulling over the problems facing the city, he cast an eye over his sprawling gardens. Even in the fading light, the grass and flowers looked withered to an unseemly brown. The big well in the middle of the garden had some water deep down, but Raman did not have the time or the energy to draw it out. He sighed and surveyed the depressing sight, swivelling round from time to time to examine a particular bush or tree.

Then, out of the corner of his eyes, Raman caught a fleeting movement in the bushes fringing the lawn. He casually threw a couple of glances in that direction, confirming his initial suspicion. Yes, there were thieves concealed in that thicket and he would have to think fast to outwit them.

By the time Raman had walked to the house, the solution had presented itself. Grinning to himself, he called out loudly for dinner. He ate his fill and then came out to the backyard to wash his hands. A quick glance at the thicket assured him that the uninvited visitors were still there. He methodically rinsed his mouth, lingering over this ritual to such an extent that Mangamma came out to enquire what the matter was.

'I was thinking,' said Raman loudly. 'You know there are thieves roaming about the city by night. Well, I don't think our valuables are safe in the house. Let's put them in a box and throw that in a well. No thief will think of looking in there—and we can sleep easy.'

Mangamma looked surprised and opened her mouth to expostulate, but Raman drew her inside with a wink. Once indoors, Raman whispered his plan to her. Mangamma was soon hard at work, fetching the heaviest, most useless household items and throwing them into an old brass box.

A short while later, Raman lugged the box to the well, sweating profusely and gasping from the weight. He hoisted it over the edge with great effort and let it fall. There was a tremendous splash as the box hit the water and settled down at the bottom of the well. Satisfied, Raman went in to rest after his labours. Soon all the lights in the house were extinguished as the household settled down for the night.

The thieves emerged, ghostlike, from the thicket, and were almost as pleased as Raman was.

'That was easy!' laughed one.

'Imagine his shock,' grinned another, 'when he finds the box missing.'

The three men set about drawing water out of the well in order to find the box. It was hard work for although the water was far down, there was quite a lot of it and the box was practically invisible at the bottom. The well would have to be emptied. So intent were the men on their task that they failed to notice a shadowy figure darting about the garden, making small burrows and channels and directing the well water to the dry plants and trees. Raman had to scoop and dig right behind the robbers, at first, to make use of the spilt water but none of them noticed or heard him. As a result, not a drop of water was wasted and the invigorating smell of wet earth made Raman inhale deeply and sigh with pleasure.

The thieves worked right through the night until one of them noticed that the sky was a shade paler and that the birds were beginning to twitter in the trees.

'Hurry!' he growled. 'We don't have much time left.'

One of the other two men secured himself with a rope and got into the well. A series of loud grunts seemed to indicate that he had found the box, and his two companions heaved him up with gusty sighs. Soon the box was on the ground, and the three thieves prepared to see the rewards of their night's labour.

The first thief sprang forward and threw back the lid. For an instant, the miscreants stared down at the motley collection, dismay dawning on their features. Then, as one, they ran towards the bushes. All was discovered—they had to flee!

Just as they neared the thicket, a voice hailed them. 'Wait a bit!' Raman called cheerfully. 'Only a few plants are left. Why don't you water them as well?'

The thieves burst through the thicket and pounded down the street right into the arms of a guard who, taking one look at their dishevelled appearance, hauled them off to jail.

Raman went back inside to catch up on lost sleep and later, informed the king about the night's events.

Krishna Devaraya was overjoyed. 'There are still a couple of them at large, Raman,' he said. 'See if you can get them as well.'

'Well, I didn't exactly go looking for them,' pointed out Raman. 'But if they come calling on me again, I'll be ready.'

For some days after this, the spate of robberies went down. But not long afterwards, Raman saw a shadowy figure in the same thicket in his garden one evening. He sat down promptly on the verandah and chatted with his wife and son as if nothing had happened.

'It's getting late,' said Mangamma at last. 'Your dinner is ready, so you better have your bath now.'

Raman got up obediently, took off his court attire and wrapped a towel round his waist. Then, to Mangamma's surprise, he carried the bucket of water over to the thicket. The water was so hot that he was surrounded by a cloud of steam.

'What stupidity is this?' she called.

'I feel like having a real hot bath out in the cold today,' was the faint reply.

Mangamma clicked her tongue in annoyance and followed her whimsical husband to the garden. Before she could say anything, however, Raman diverted her attention with a few hilarious jokes and some court gossip, too. Meanwhile, he kept splashing the water erratically about— occasionally a little bit over himself, but mainly into the thicket.

The thief sat still in the thicket, unable to stir for fear of being detected. He couldn't even shriek when the hot water splashed on him at regular intervals and sloshed down his neck.

Finally, Raman scooped out the last bit of water and threw it on his wife. Mangamma let out a bloodcurdling scream, wrung her hands and stormed, 'Are you mad? Or is this some stupid childish prank? You've been wasting precious water—spilling it all over the place—and now my clothes are soaked! What do you ...?'

Raman chortled and then said loudly, 'Just because I've thrown a little water at you, you get hysterical. But think of that poor gentleman in the thicket. I've emptied almost half of this very hot water on his head and he hasn't said a word!'

Mangamma stared at her husband, flabbergasted. Then, all at once, a bedraggled figure emerged from the thicket and threw himself at Raman's feet.

'Forgive me!' cried the thief. 'I will never rob anyone ever again—if you'll just let me go.'

'You'll have to do better than that, my good fellow,' retorted Raman, calmly rubbing himself dry. 'You and the rest of your gang had better leave this town at once—or else you will face the consequences.'

The thief stared at him.

'You know I can catch you all, don't you?' added Raman briskly.

The thief nodded wildly and began babbling a series of promises, chiefly that the city would be rid of robbers by that night.

And so it was.

Needless to say, Raman was richer by a couple of purses of gold.

Less or More

Raman clearly had the keenest wit and the sharpest mind at the Vijayanagara court but there were rare instances when he felt threatened by others. And the challenge was nowhere more evident than when it came from Ranga Sani, the most beautiful courtesan in the city.

Ranga Sani was not merely beautiful and talented. She also had one of the most astute and scholarly minds in Vijayanagara. She could easily challenge and defeat established scholars on any subject she chose.

And in the realm of logic, she had no parallel. It is no wonder that Raman feared her above all others and waited apprehensively for the day when he would be decisively trounced by her.

And so it came about that Ranga Sani, thirsting for some kind of intellectual challenge, proclaimed before the king her desire to have a test of logic with any of the scholars at the court.

'If I lose,' she said, her eyes flashing, 'I shall give the victor half of my wealth. But if I win, then these scholars will have to carry me around in a chariot and publicly acknowledge their defeat at my hands.'

The king immediately looked at the assembled scholars but there was no response. Most of his eight court gems were either exchanging shifty glances or looking fixedly at the ground.

'Well, come on,' said Krishna Devaraya impatiently. 'Will no one take up Ranga Sani's challenge?'

The courtesan had a jubilant expression on her face, as if she was already tasting victory. Then, all at once, Raman stood up.

'I'll take on the challenge,' he said slowly. 'But I need some time to prepare.'

The king sat back, satisfied, while the other scholars, rescued from their predicament, cast pitying glances at Raman. How would he ever defeat Ranga

Sani in logic? It was a near-impossible task!

The courtesan looked appraisingly at Raman and then left the court. There was no doubt in her mind that she would defeat the jester.

Meanwhile, Raman wondered whether he had been too impulsive in offering to pit his skills against Ranga Sani. For all he knew, a public humiliation was round the corner and he had more or less asked for it!

While brooding over the problem, Raman made his way, quite unwittingly, to the street where Ranga Sani lived. A student of his, Bhushana, happened to be passing by and promptly hurried across to greet him.

It was then that Ranga Sani emerged from her house to buy some firewood from a vendor on the street. The vendor was clearly in a hurry to get away and the transaction was concluded at lightning speed. The bundle of wood was hastily deposited at the courtesan's doorstep. Ranga Sani tried to lift the wood but it was too heavy.

At this point, Raman whispered something in Bhushana's ear and sent him to her.

'Should I help you with this bundle?' asked the boy.

'Oh, yes,' said Ranga Sani gratefully. 'Please carry this in for me.'

'Will I get anything in return?' smiled Bhushana.

'Of course,' said Ranga Sani briskly. 'I'll give you a little jaggery to eat.'

'I don't want a little jaggery,' said Bhushana. 'I want more jaggery to eat.'

'Yes, yes,' said the courtesan impatiently. 'I'll give you more. Now just bring this bundle inside.'

Bhushana did as he was told. Once the bundle was safely deposited where she wanted it, he asked for the jaggery.

Ranga Sani gave him a lump but the boy immediately asked for more. When she gave him some more jaggery, he demanded still more. This went on for quite a while, with the courtesan growing increasingly perplexed by Bhushana's insatiable appetite for jaggery.

Finally, she scraped out the last bits from the storage vessel and said firmly, 'Look, this is all that is left. You've eaten up my entire stock of jaggery.'

'No, I want more jaggery,' said Bhushana obstinately.

'Are you crazy?' demanded Ranga Sani, unsure whether to humour the boy or to send him away summarily. She decided on the former course and sent her servant to the shop for more jaggery. However, even this appeared insufficient for Bhushana who kept up his chant of 'I want more jaggery.'

Ranga Sani lost her temper and shouted at Bhushana but he would not budge from his stance. She tried to push him out of the house but he stood on the doorstep and kept up his demand in a loud and insistent tone.

In no time at all, a crowd gathered around them. The boy seemed completely unruffled by the audience and continued to plaintively demand more jaggery.

'Come back inside!' ordered Ranga Sani, embarrassed to be a public spectacle.

'I want more jaggery!' wailed Bhushana.

Someone in the crowd suggested that they take the matter to the king. So the entire crowd moved to the court, appealing to Krishna Devaraya to settle the issue.

'This is a ridiculous situation,' observed the king. 'I can't think of any way to resolve it.' He turned to the court scholars. 'Can any of you think of a solution?'

Raman sprang up. 'I can settle this matter but on one condition. Ranga Sani must admit that she cannot solve this problem and that she accepts defeat in this regard.'

The courtesan was one step short of tearing her hair out by the roots. 'All right, I accept my defeat!' she exclaimed vexedly. 'Now *you* solve the problem, if you can.'

Raman turned calmly to Bhushana. 'How much jaggery do you want?'

'I want more jaggery,' said the boy promptly.

Raman produced two pieces of jaggery—one tiny lump and the other considerably bigger—and held them out in his palm. 'Of the two, which is more jaggery?' he asked Bhushana.

Bhushana pointed to the larger lump, took it and then left the court.

Raman swung round to Ranga Sani. 'Well, haven't you just lost the test on logic?' he asked softly.

Ranga Sani struck her forehead. 'You tricked me!' she cried. Then she smiled and shrugged her shoulders. 'Yes, you're right. I *have* lost the challenge. So I owe you half of my wealth now.'

Raman heaved a huge sigh of relief and Krishna Devaraya, realising—with rare perception—just what was going on in the jester's mind, smiled at him and shook his head. He had come perilously close to being toppled from his throne but had salvaged the situation in his usual inimitable style. Raman, to the world at large, was quite simply unbeatable!

Food for Thought

Krishna Devaraya was a great patron of the arts. Among his favourites was Raja Varma, a truly exceptional artist, who was provided every imaginable luxury while drawing the king's portrait.

Raja Varma was a gentle, unassuming man, who laboured over his task. When at last it was ready, the king was thrilled by the astonishingly lifelike quality of the painting. 'There is not one feature that is not exactly like mine,' he declared joyfully. 'This is the best portrait I have seen in years. What else can you draw?'

Raja Varma shyly displayed the range of his repertoire that included beautiful images of characters from the epics and realistic ones of contemporary people.

'You are an absolute genius,' the king pronounced. 'Ask for anything you want and you will get it.'

The modest artist was overwhelmed by this offer and didn't quite know what to say. There wasn't anything that he really craved for. His only desire was to be left alone to get on with his paintings, and absorb himself in the world of lines and colours. So he wracked his brains for an appropriate reply.

However, before he could utter a single word, the king snapped his fingers.

'I know what to give you,' he said exultantly. 'You will become my chief minister as of today.'

Raja Varma stood stock-still in horror. He experienced such sharp pangs of uneasiness that he felt it was safer not to move even a finger. He tried to summon up words of refusal that wouldn't sound rude or offensive but he failed.

And so, he agreed to his new job and conscientiously set about trying to learn the ropes, feeling utterly miserable from the very first minute. However, Raja Varma's genius was only artistic and he had no talent for being an administrator at all! In next to no time, there was complete chaos in the city, thanks to his hasty, illogical decisions and total absence of managerial skills.

Yet, since he was also an intelligent man, he was well aware that he was making a mess of things, but had no idea how to remedy the situation. He spent his days in a haze of misery and dived back to the comfort of his paintings whenever he could squeeze out the time.

Ripples of discontent grew in ever-widening circles but the people could not be more vocal about their views for fear of offending the king.

The king's liking for the artist, however, remained constant. He dismissed all rumours and contrary advice regarding the latter with an airy wave. So when all else failed, the town elders and some senior scholars and ministers like Allasani Peddanna and Thimmarusu decided to pin their hopes on Raman in a final bid to salvage the situation.

The jester heard them out patiently. He said, 'Don't worry. Things are in my hands now—and I will find a way out of this muddle.'

For a few weeks after this, there was no sign of any change. The elders were beginning to wonder whether Raman had forgotten his promise. However, they could not get the jester to divulge his plans, if any.

Shortly thereafter, Raman invited the king and

some important ministers to lunch at his house. When they willingly accepted, he tracked down the best carpenter in the city and gave him the job of preparing a grand feast for the special guests.

On the appointed day, Raman's guests arrived, smacking their lips in anticipation of a sumptuous meal. The carpenter was hard at work, putting the finishing touches to his dishes.

'What has been prepared, Raman?' the king queried eagerly.

'Wait and see, sir,' answered Raman. 'But I promise you—this is one feast you won't forget in a hurry.'

The food was served on beautiful platters and the guests reached for their first mouthfuls.

The king took a huge bite and then suddenly began to gasp and choke. 'Water!' he cried urgently. 'Give me some water quickly!'

By this time, cries of disgust echoed round the table with everyone retching or screaming for water in a panic-stricken chorus.

'Raman, this food is horrible!' shrieked the king, his face an interesting shade of red. 'It's too hot, too salty, and grossly undercooked! Just look at these potatoes—they're so hard you have to crack them open like nuts!' He paused to take more gulps of water and then went on with renewed indignation,

'Who has cooked this food? Is this your idea of a feast? Do you want us all to die or something?'

Raman waited for the uproar to subside. He looked extremely contrite and spoke with folded hands. 'Forgive me, sir. I will introduce the cook to you, with your permission.' He ushered the bewildered carpenter forward. 'This is the best carpenter in Vijayanagara. His work is unparalleled. I gave him the job of cooking the food today.'

The king glared at the hapless carpenter and then, quite unexpectedly, his mouth began to twitch. 'Are you crazy, Raman? He might be a brilliant worker on wood but does that mean he is a good cook?'

'But, sir,' Raman murmured, 'if an artist can be the chief minister, then why can't a carpenter be a cook?'

The king glared balefully at him for a few minutes but Raman bore the look without flinching.

Then Krishna Devaraya lowered his eyes and shook his head ruefully. 'You are right, Raman. I know what you are trying to tell me.'

The king went back to the palace, along with his hungry entourage, fully prepared to relieve Raja Varma from his post as soon as possible.

The following morning, though, Raja Varma presented himself before the king and, without any preamble, begged to be rid of his post.

The king was surprised and a trifle embarrassed. 'But is it because ... I mean, did you hear about Raman's ...?'

'Sir,' interjected Raja Varma with unexpected firmness, 'I am no good as a chief minister. My profession is that of an artist—so please let me go back to being one.' 'All right—if that is what you want,' replied the king.

As he left the court, Raja Varma threw a smile of heartfelt gratitude in Raman's direction for making his task so much easier. He had never felt happier in years!

The Old Man
and the Seed

Although Raman was very well known in and around
Vijayanagara, it thrilled him to learn that his fame
had spread all the way to the court of the Mughal
emperor, Babur, at Delhi. One of Babur's courtiers
had praised Raman's wit and wisdom, dubbing him
the best jester in the world. The emperor was instantly
intrigued. He wrote to Krishna Devaraya, requesting
him to send Raman to Delhi for a month so that he
could verify the truth for himself.

Raman preened himself and went about with a huge, satisfied smirk on his face. Mangamma flitted about, torn between pride at her husband's fame and anxiety at the thought of his sojourn at Delhi.

As the date of Raman's departure neared, even the king seemed to catch some of Mangamma's anxiety and became strangely jittery. 'Look, Raman,' he said. 'You have simply *got* to impress that emperor and get some reward from him. I don't want him to think that you shine here only because Vijayanagara is a place for mediocre people. If you get a reward from him, I will give you a thousand gold coins.' Then he paused, 'But if you don't,' he continued, his mind assailed by horrific visions of dishonour, 'then I will be forced to get your head shaved as a mark of disgrace and drive you away from here.'

No frown marred Raman's brow when he heard this dire pronouncement. The candid look in his eyes increased the king's discomfiture. The latter said, in a slightly less abrasive tone, 'Apparently the emperor's attendant gives a bag containing a hundred gold coins to anyone whose words the emperor approves of. Just try and get one of those bags at least.'

'Is there any doubt about that?' Raman queried mildly.

Meanwhile, Babur was issuing instructions of a very different sort to his courtiers. 'I am going to test

Tenali Raman in a very thorough manner,' he announced. 'So I don't want any of you to laugh at his jokes or appreciate anything he says—or induce me to do either. The person who breaks this order will be beheaded.' Then he chuckled. 'That jester will not get a reward very easily in *this* court.'

Once at Delhi, Raman, for all his worldly-wise ways, was deeply impressed by the pomp of the court and by the charismatic emperor. He was received with great ceremony and given every conceivable comfort.

Yet there was one thing that puzzled him. Though he was at his scintillating best before Babur, there was not the slightest sign of amusement or appreciation from him—or from the rest of the court, for that matter. It was exhausting and difficult to be witty and entertaining when the audience was so uniformly dour and unsmiling. It was like throwing stones down a deep valley, Raman mused. You didn't see them hit their mark nor did you hear any sound. These northerners, he thought sourly, do not know how to laugh. Yet he kept up his efforts for an entire fortnight, though he felt his jokes becoming feebler with every passing day.

On the sixteenth day, Raman did not attend court.

The emperor smiled to himself as he set out on his daily walk the following morning. 'Maybe he has already acknowledged defeat. So much for that jester's skills!' Then he drove all thoughts of Raman from his mind and concentrated on the sights around him, occasionally throwing a remark or two over his shoulder to his attendant.

A short while later, Babur spotted an old Muslim with a flowing grey beard by the roadside. Though the man was bent with age, he was earnestly trying to plant a seed in a pit that he had evidently dug.

The emperor walked up to the man. 'Grandfather,' he said, in tones of polite concern. 'What are you doing?'

'I'm planting a mango tree,' replied the old man in a quavering voice. 'Once it grows, the fruits will sell very well.'

Babur frowned. 'But you are old and might not live to eat its fruits. So what use is the tree to you?'

'God is great,' was the pious answer. 'After all, he made my father plant trees whose fruits I ate. And if my father planted trees so that I could enjoy the fruits, why can't I plant trees for others to enjoy their fruits?'

'That was very well said,' said Babur thoughtfully. He signalled to his attendant who promptly deposited a bag containing a hundred gold coins in the old man's lap.

The old man was clearly overcome and wiped tears from his eyes. 'God is great,' he said in a trembling voice, 'and so is the emperor. All men get their crops after the trees grow but I have got mine even before I planted this tree. See—the very thought of doing good to others brings us such good results.'

The emperor clasped his hands and nodded approvingly. 'Again, very well said!'

The attendant gave the old man another bag of gold coins.

The latter now became effusive. 'God is truly great!' he exclaimed. 'When this tree grows, it will give only one crop a year. But with God's grace and the emperor's goodness, it has given me two crops on the very day that it was planted.'

'Extremely well said,' pronounced Babur, struck anew by the old man's profundity. Another bag of gold coins exchanged hands.

'Come on,' Babur smiled at his attendant. 'Let's be on our way or this old man will empty my treasury.'

'Wait a minute,' called the old man.

The emperor turned round sharply, for the man's feeble tone had been replaced by an extremely robust and vigorous one. Raman had thrown away his beard and Babur stared at him, dumbfounded.

'God is great,' intoned Raman solemnly, 'and so is the emperor—and Raman has won his praise thrice now in five minutes.'

Babur shook his head ruefully and smiled. 'You deserve all your fame, Raman. You are truly a very clever man. Take your rewards and tell your king about your success here—and also tell him that he is a lucky man to have you in his court.'

And so, Raman went back to Vijayanagara—a genuinely relieved man—and gave a painstaking account of his deeds to Krishna Devaraya.

'I suppose I *am* lucky to have you,' murmured the king, 'but don't get a swollen head on that account!'

Pocketing his reward of a thousand gold coins, Raman flashed a cheeky grin of triumph at the king.